LYNACIA'S
DRAGON

L. M. Walsh

ISBN 978-1-0980-8841-5 (paperback)
ISBN 978-1-63961-691-6 (hardcover)
ISBN 978-1-0980-8916-0 (digital)

Christian Faith Publishing, Inc.
832 Park Avenue
Meadville, PA 16335
www.christianfaithpublishing.com

Printed in the United States of America

Who looks outside dreams, who looks inside awakens.

—Carl Jung

This book is dedicated to: my son Jason and his wife Kellie, my daughter Sonya and my grandchildren: Kailyn, Dante, Christopher, Noah, Nyla, Anaya and Delanie. And of course my great grandson, Jase.

Once upon a time in a nearby but often overlooked place was the land of the Enchanted Mountains. Deep within the Enchanted Mountains, there lived a young girl named Lynacia. She was full of energy, life, and curiosity, and lived happily as one with her mountain surroundings. However, inside her was a deep and unfulfilled longing to see outside her land and have adventures, which she was not free to do. The one thing that Lynacia lacked was freedom to explore beyond her land.

It was told that, when Lynacia was a very young girl, her mother had placed a spell of protection over her so that she would never leave

the safety of the Enchanted Mountains. Her mother truly believed she was protecting her, but, in reality, her mother's protective nature had created a curse. For Lynacia longed for discovery and travel, and not being able to explore outside her land caused her much sadness and longing for what she could not do.

The spell that Lynacia's mother had cast placed a dragon to watch and ensure that Lynacia never left. She tried many times to venture out, but each time, the dragon would surface and overwhelm her, taking over her mind and body until she surrendered the attempt. What was meant to protect her imprisoned her.

As many travelers passed through the land, Lynacia would find herself intrigued by the diversity of their ways, their dress, and especially their stories. Lynacia would listen from an undetected distance as they shared their stories around campsites. She loved to imagine what it would be like to visit such places and have such adventures. Oh, how she would love to do so.

On rare occasion, when her curiosity was stronger than her fear, she would approach the travelers to ask questions about their travels. They always welcomed her as they found her interest and curiosity enchanting. When asked where she had been or why she does not go, Lynacia would never reveal the truth. She would just reply that she hopes to one day. She really hopes to.

Often, young male travelers, so taken with Lynacia, would try to convince her to join them in their travels. There was even an occasion when she wanted so badly to go that she told the suitor about the curse, thinking maybe he would fight the dragon and free her. But he was not interested in fighting a dragon. She was deeply saddened by this, as she had read of brave men killing dragons, and thought it could have been her opportunity to be freed. Even though she tried to convince herself that she must accept her confinement in the Enchanted Mountains, she still found herself secretly hoping to be rescued.

After that, whenever the subject of leaving came up, Lynacia would promptly depart, never telling anyone again of the curse. She had become very skillful at quickly running away from people whenever they grew too close or asked too many questions of her. She was afraid to ever again dream for one willing or brave enough to slay her dragon.

It was in the spring of Lynacia's twenty-third birthday that a handsome prince traveled through the Enchanted Mountains on his way home from a wedding celebration. His second cousin, a